ISBN 978-1-7335175-3-9

All rights reserved. Published by Sweetberry Books
Visit us on the web! www.sweetberrybooks.com

10 9 8 7 6 5 4 3 2 1
Printed in the U.S.A.

# THE GREATEST GIFT IS NOT BEING AFRAID TO QUESTION.

Ruby Dee

Black American Actress, Poet, Playwright, Screenwriter,

Journalist & Civil Rights Activist

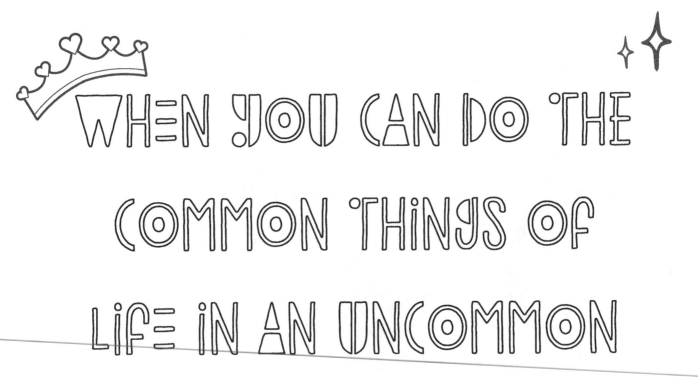

WHEN YOU CAN DO THE COMMON THINGS OF LIFE IN AN UNCOMMON WAY, YOU WILL COMMAND THE ATTENTION OF THE WORLD.

George Washington Carver

Black American Agricultural Scientist & Inventor

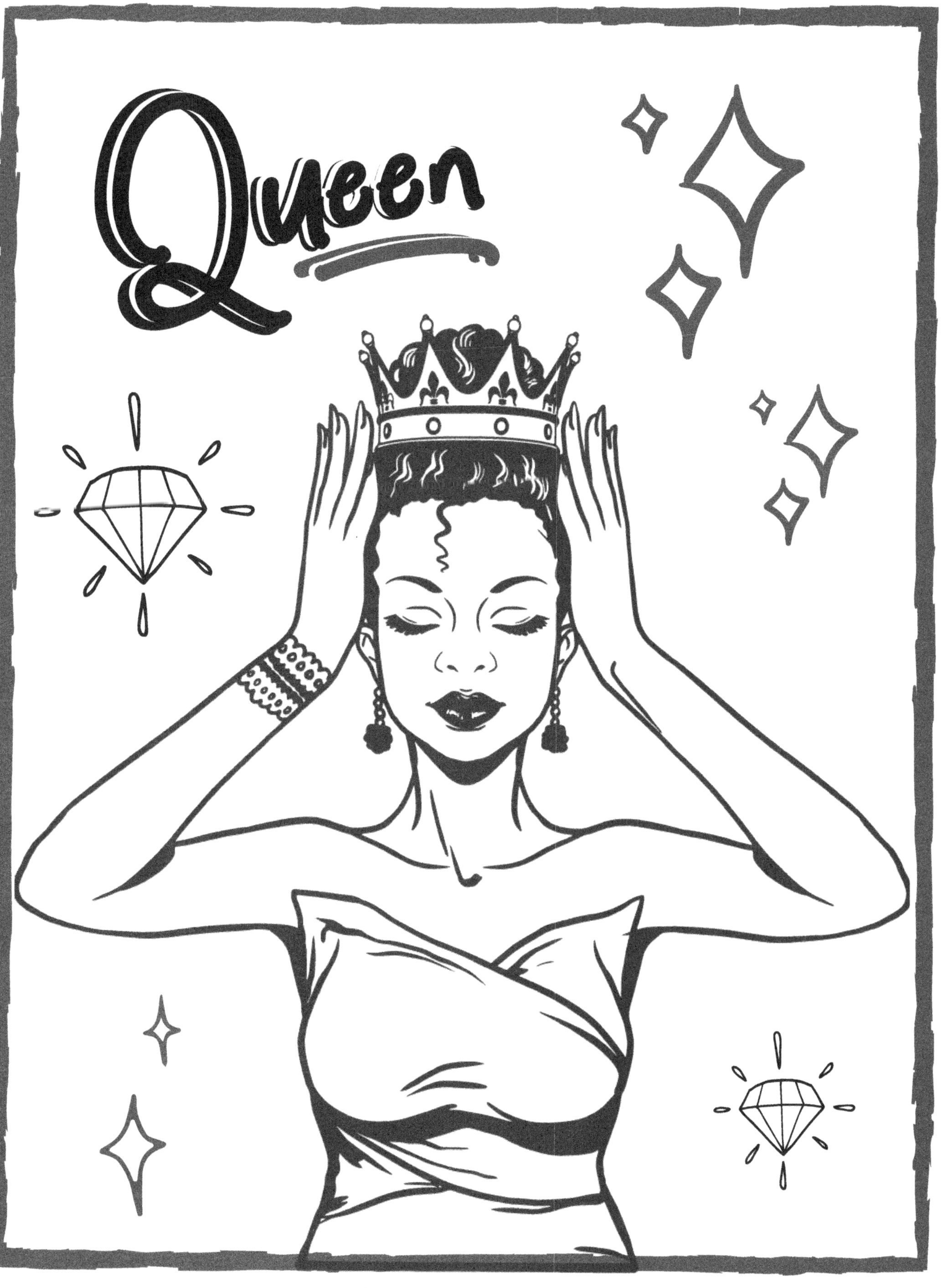
Queen

# Be the best version of yourself in anything you do.

# You don't have to live anybody else's story.

Stephen Curry

Black American Professional Basketball Player

# THE BIGGEST ADVENTURE YOU CAN EVER TAKE IS TO LIVE THE LIFE OF YOUR DREAMS.

Oprah Winfrey

Black American Television Host and Producer, Actress, Media Executive & Philanthropist

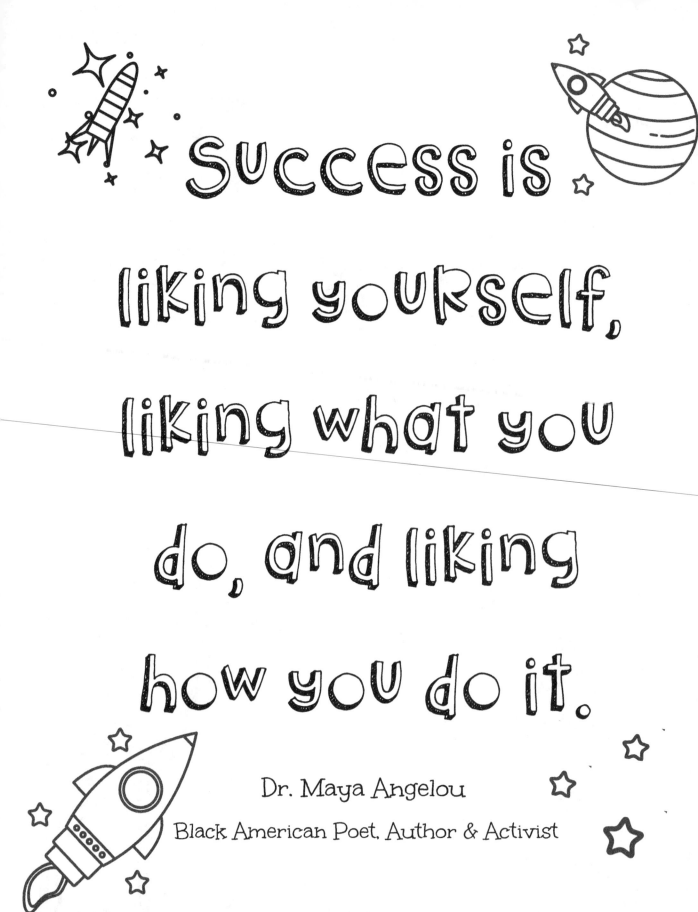

Success is liking yourself, liking what you do, and liking how you do it.

Dr. Maya Angelou

Black American Poet, Author & Activist

# You are

# your best

# thing.

## Toni Morrison

### Black American Novelist, Essayist, Editor & Professor

# I was built this way for a reason, so I'm going to use it.

Simone Biles

Black American Olympic and World Champion Gymnist

# IT ISN'T WHERE

# YOU COME FROM;

 # IT'S WHERE

# YOU'RE GOING

# THAT COUNTS.

Ella Fitzgerald

Black American Grammy Award Winning Jazz Singer

IMAGINE WHAT A HARMONIOUS WORLD COULD BE IF EVERY SINGLE PERSON, BOTH YOUNG AND OLD, SHARED A LITTLE OF WHAT HE IS GOOD AT

Quincy Jones

Black American Music, Film and Television Producer,
Instrumentalist, Songwriter & Composer

You have to believe in yourself when no one else does ... that makes you a winner right there.

Venus Williams

Black American Olymipic Tennis Champion

 Never underestimate the power of dreams.

The potential for greatness lives within each of us.

 Wilma Rudolph

Black American Olymipic Track and Field Champion

# The whole woRld opened to me when I leaRned to Read.

Mary McLeod Bethune

Black American Educator, Stateswoman, Philanthropist,
Humanitarian & Civil Rights Activist

# EMBRACE WHAT

# MAKES YOU

# UNIQUE, EVEN IF

# IT MAKES OTHERS

# UNCOMFORTABLE.

Janelle Monae

Black American Singer, Songwriter, Actress & Producer

If You don't Like Something, Change it.  If You Can't Change it, Change  Your attitude.

Dr. Maya Angelou

Black American Poet, Author & Activist

# NEVER AGREE TO SURRENDER YOUR DREAMS.

Jesse Jackson

Black American Civil Rights Activist, Minister & Politician

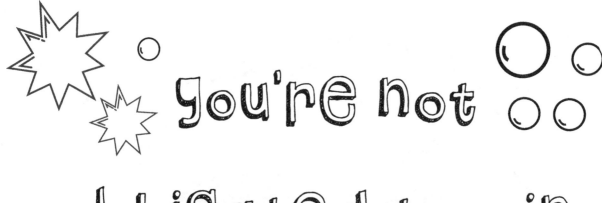

You're not obligated to win. You're obligated to KEEP TRYING to do the best you can every day.

Marian Wright Edelman

Black American Lawyer & Activist for Children's Rights

# The Challenge is in the moment; the time is always now.

James Baldwin

Black American Novelist, Playwright, Essayist, Poet & Activist

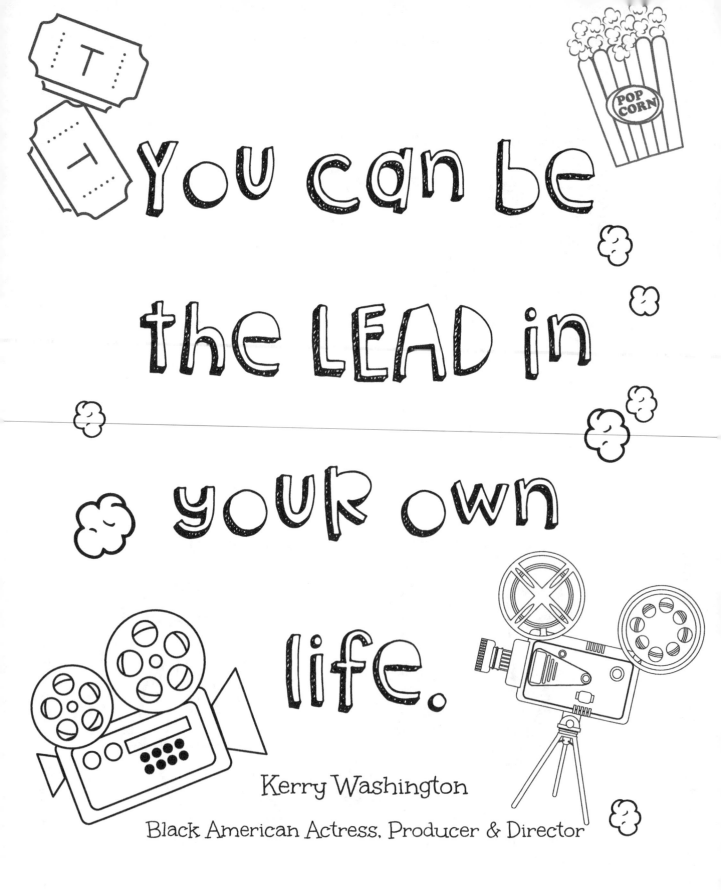

You can be the LEAD in your own life.

Kerry Washington

Black American Actress, Producer & Director

# MAGIC LIES IN CHALLENGING WHAT SEEMS IMPOSSIBLE.

Carol Moseley Braun
Black American Diplomat, Politician & Lawyer

# THE TIME IS ALWAYS RIGHT TO DO WHAT IS RIGHT

Martin Luther King, Jr.

Black American Minister, Activist & Civil Rights Leader

what you're

THINKING

is what you're

BECOMING.

Muhammad Ali

Black American Champion Boxer, Activist & Philantropist

# Let GRaTiTUDE be the Pillow upon which you kneel to say your nightly prayer.

Dr. Maya Angelou
Black American Poet, Author & Activist

# YOU MUST BE BOLD, BRAVE, AND COURAGEOUS AND FIND A WAY... TO GET IN THE WAY.

John Lewis

Black American Politician & Civil Rights Leader

 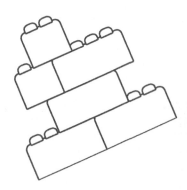

# It is easier to build strong children than to repair broken men.

Frederick Douglass

Black American Activist, Author, Speaker and Escaped Slave

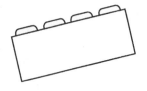 

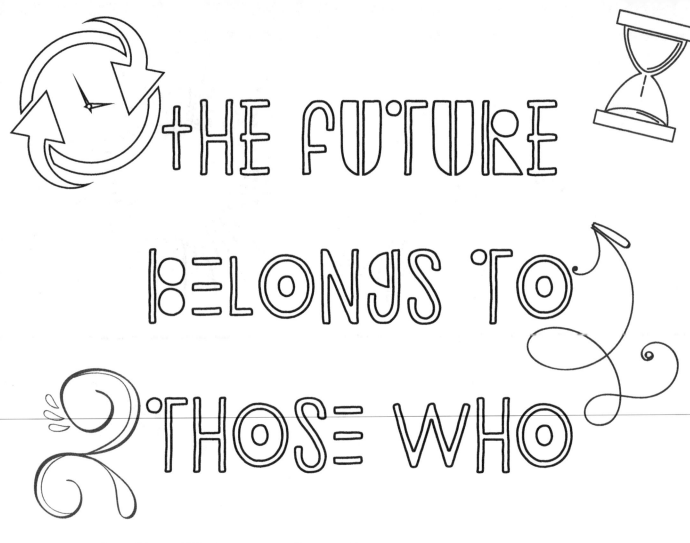

THE FUTURE BELONGS TO THOSE WHO PREPARE FOR IT TODAY.

Malcom X

Black American Minister & Civil Rights Activist

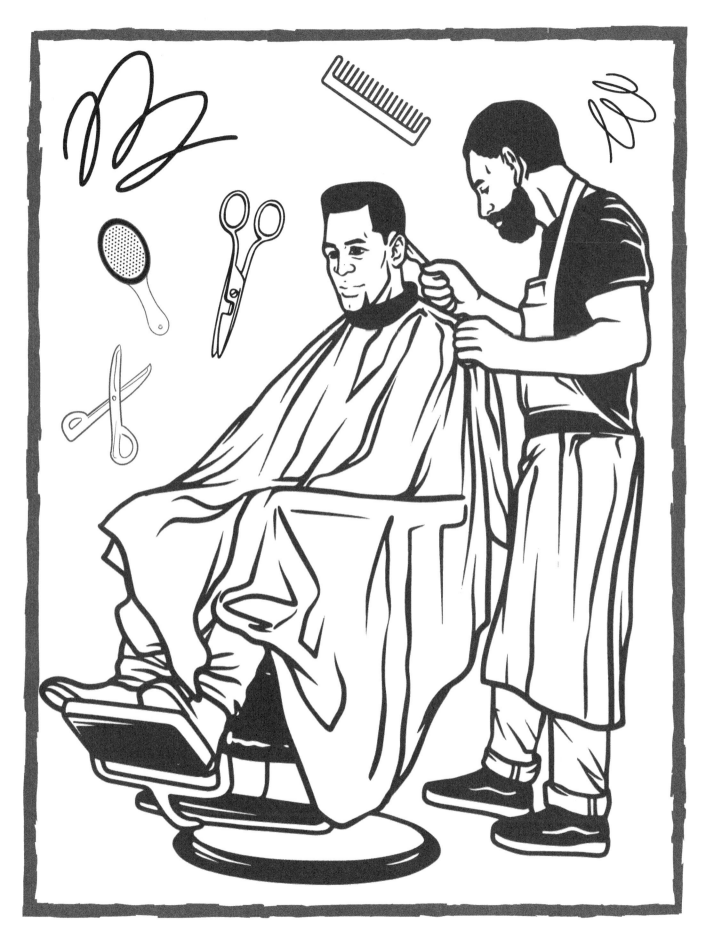

# Like what you do, and then

# you will do your best.

Katherine Johnson

Black American Mathematician & Pivotal NASA Employee

# YOU HAVE WITHIN YOU THE STRENGTH, THE PATIENCE, AND THE PASSION TO REACH FOR THE STARS TO CHANGE THE WORLD.

Harriet Tubman
Conductor on the Underground Railroad

whatever we BELIVE about ourselves And Our ability comes TRUE for us.

Susan L. Taylor

Black American Writer, Journalist & former Editor-In-Chief

Don't sit down and wait for the opportunities to come. Get up and make them.

Madame C. J. Walker

Black American Entrepreneur, Philanthropist, & Political and Social Activist.

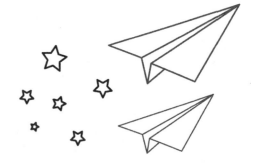

# KEEP GOING, no Matter WHat.

Reginald F. Lewis

First Black American to Build a Billion Dollar Business

# DON't COUNT tHE DAYS MAKE tHE DAYS COUNT.

Muhammad Ali

Blsck American Heavyweight Championship Boxer

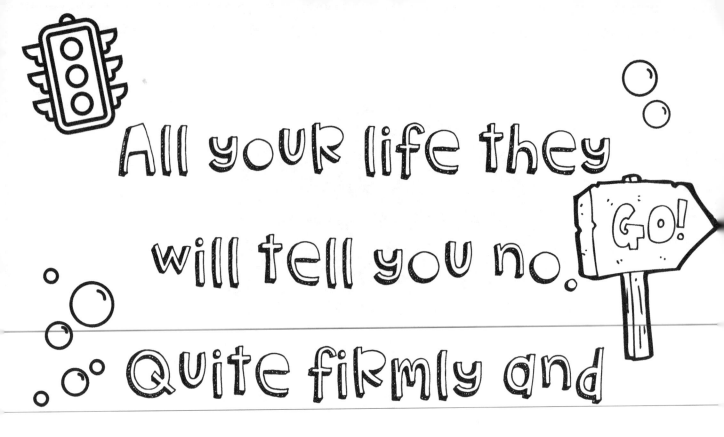

All your life they will tell you no. Quite firmly and very quickly. And you will tell them yes.

LeBron James

Black American Professional Basketball Player

# THE MOST IMPORTANT THING IS TO BELIEVE IN YOURSELF AND KNOW THAT YOU CAN DO IT.

Gabby Douglas

Black American Artistic Gymnast

# Always Stay TRUE to Yourself and never Let what Somebody else Says distract You from YOUR GoALS.

Michelle Obama

Black American Writer, Lawyer and Former U.S. First Lady

The moment you give up, is the moment you let someone else win.

Kobe Bryant

Black American Professional Basketball Player

# START WHERE YOU ARE, WITH WHAT YOU HAVE.

George Washington Carver

Black American Scientist and Inventor

# Know
## what sparks the
# LIGHT in you
## so that YOU,
## in your own way
## can ILLUMINATe the
# WORLD.

Oprah Winfrey

First Black Female Billionare

# Never
# be Limited
## by other people's
## Limited
# imaginations.

Dr. Mae Jemison
First Black American Female Astronaut

Try to be a
rainbow
in someone's
Cloud.

Dr. Maya Angelou
Black American Poet,
Author & Activist

THERE ARE BILLION BOYS AND GIRLS WHO ARE YOUNG, GIFTED AND BLACK AND THAT'S A FACT!

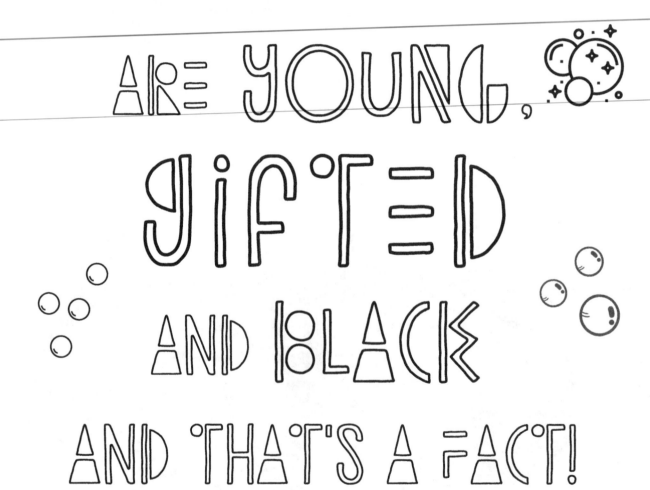

Performed by Nina Simone
Known as the "Singer of the Black Revoloution"

CHASE YOUR DREAMS. INSTEAD OF RUNNING FROM YOUR FEARS.

Anonymous

# Every great Dream begins with a dreamer.

Harriet Tubman
Conductor of the Underground Railroad

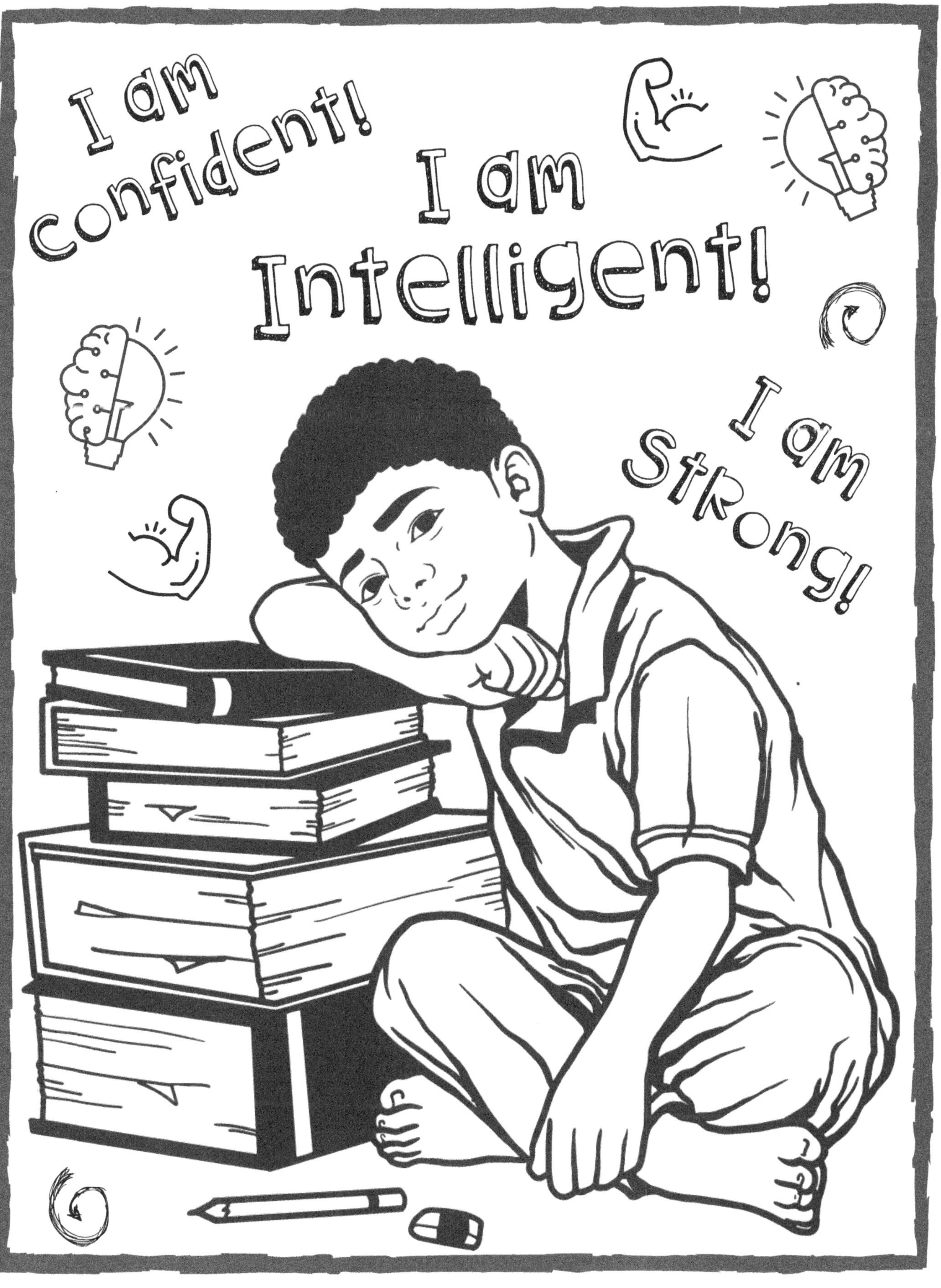
I am Confident!
I am Intelligent!
I am Strong!

Find the Good.

It's all

Around you.

Jessie Owens
Black American Olympic Gold Medalist

Stretch your mind and FLY.

Whitney M. Young Jr.
Black American Civil Rights Activist

# MY faVoRite qUotE:

# My masterpiece:

Made in the USA
Middletown, DE
24 July 2023

35686923R00053

# THE X TAILS

## SKATEBOARD AT

**WRITTEN BY**
L.A. Fielding

**ILLUSTRATED BY**
Victor Guiza

Library and Archives Canada Cataloguing in Publication

Fielding, L. A. (Lawrence Anthony), 1977-, author
Skateboard at Monster Ramp / author: L.A. Fielding ; illustrator: Victor Guiza.

(The X-tails)
Issued in print and electronic formats.
ISBN 978-0-9937135-5-2 (pbk.).

I. Guiza, Victor, illustrator  II. Title.  III. Series: Fielding, L. A. (Lawrence Anthony), 1977- . X tails.

PS8611.I362S52 2014          jC813'.6          C2014-901968-8          C2014-901969-6

Design and text layout by Margaret Cogswell
www.spiderbuddydesigns.com

I dedicate this book to my zoober-cool wife, Corrie,
and my two zoober-awesome kids, Colton and Dylann.

Big thanks to my family and friends who
have been so supportive and have helped to
make the X-tails become a reality.

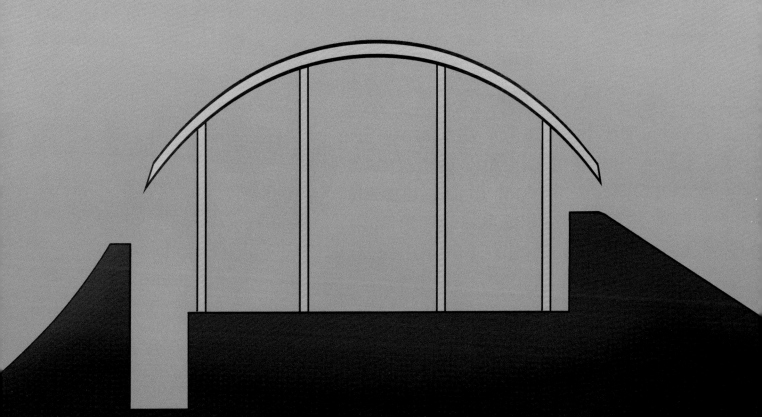

# MEET THE X-TAILS!

## WISDOM

The smart and responsible lion who is the natural leader of the X-tails. He is a master at solving problems and can fix almost anything. Wisdom loves to **"ROOaaaRRRR!"** when he is having fun.

## CHARM

The cute and bubbly kangaroo. She loves the spotlight and performing at contests in front of big crowds. Her kangaroo legs are perfect for jumping high and pedaling fast. When Charm is really happy, you will see her **HOP** around or **THUMP** her foot with a big smile.

# CRASH

The clumsy, messy, and very goofy hippo. Crash usually finds himself in all sorts of trouble and is thankful that his X-tail friends are always there when he needs them. You can't help but laugh with Crash at the many silly things he does, especially when he bellows

**"GaaaWHOOOOmPHaaaaa!"**

# FLIGHT

The strong and fearless rocker gorilla. Flight not only plays the air guitar but also loves to play on any jump he can find. Although he is really big and hairy, this gorilla is a gentle giant. You know Flight is ready for air time when you hear him grunt

**"OOOHHHH, OOOHHHH, OOOHHHH!"**

# Dazzle

The tough and brave bear who is a tomboy at heart. The boys have difficulty keeping up with Dazzle. And good luck trying to slow her down! She has a big grin, and you will often hear her friendly growl, **"GRRRRR!"**

# MISCHIEF

The practical joker of the bunch. You know Mischief is up to something sneaky when you see his mischievous grin. He is a little short for a wolf, so be careful you don't confuse him with a fox—he doesn't like that much. But being small always works to his advantage. You will hear Mischief howl when he is excited. **"aaaaWHOOOOO!"**

And we can't forget about the X-van, which takes the X-tails to the mountains, ocean, BMX tracks, and skateboard parks. This off-road machine can go anywhere and easily fits all of the X-tails' gear. Wisdom the Lion is always the driver of the X-van.

THE X-VAN

howled Mischief the Wolf. "The Monster Ramp Contest is almost here! I can't wait—this is my chance to become the skateboard champion!"

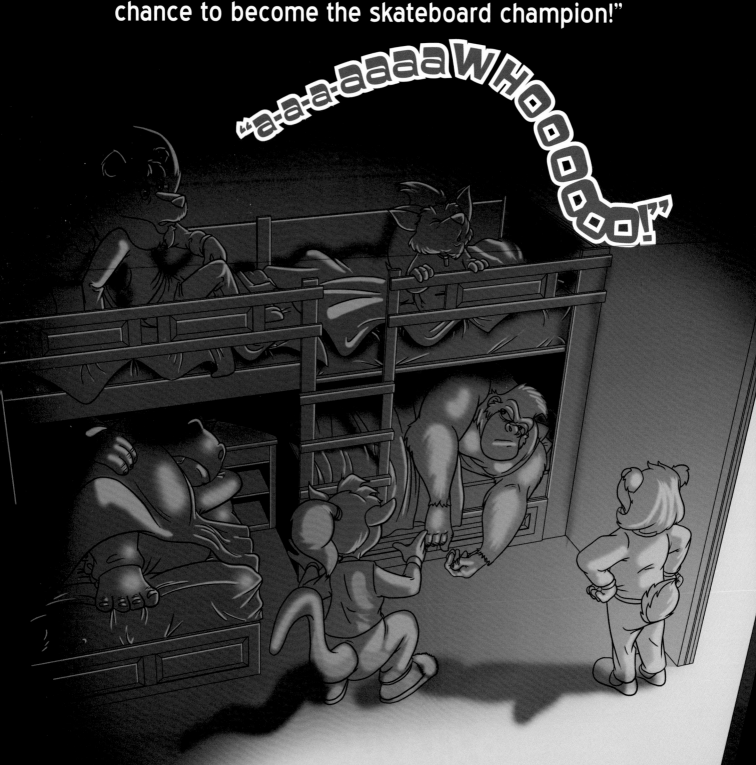

"Mischief, PAWLEEEEAAASE stop howling," begged Wisdom the Lion. "I know you're excited about tomorrow, but it's way past our bedtime. The top skateboarders in the world will be there along with last year's champion, Streak the Panther. To skateboard at our best, we need a good night's sleep."

The wide-eyed wolf did everything he could to be quiet.

He tried holding his breath.

He tried counting sheep on skateboards.

He even tried biting his pillow, but that only made a feathery mess.

Nothing worked. Mischief howled all night long!

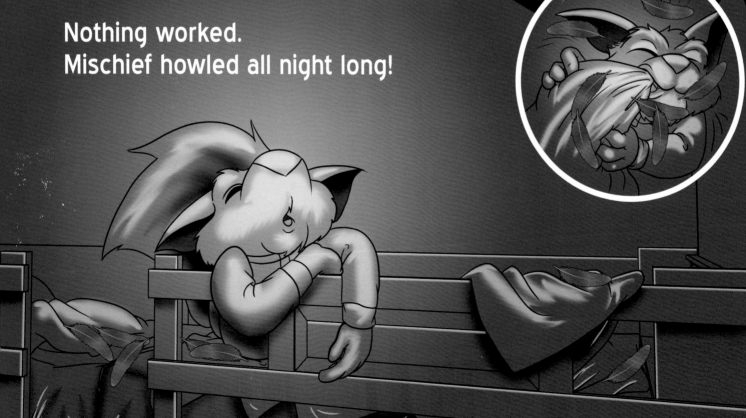

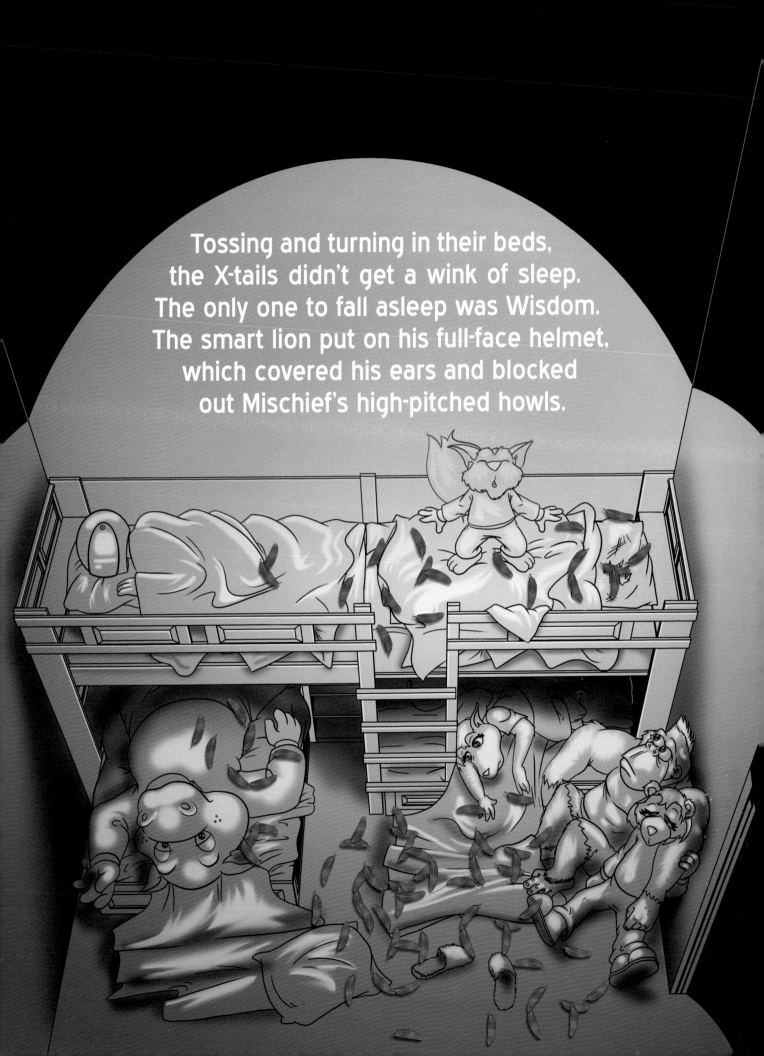

Tossing and turning in their beds,
the X-tails didn't get a wink of sleep.
The only one to fall asleep was Wisdom.
The smart lion put on his full-face helmet,
which covered his ears and blocked
out Mischief's high-pitched howls.

The next morning, Wisdom was smiling and singing, but the rest of the X-tails were sluggish and sleepy. Even Mischief was quiet and not up to his usual practical jokes. They moved around the house in slow motion.

Wisdom had to load ALL of their skateboards and ALL of their helmets and pads into the X-van. And then he waited and waited . . .

Hours later, the X-tails finally arrived at the Monster Ramp Contest. They were late! Hustling and bustling, they leaped out of the X-van and rushed into the stadium.

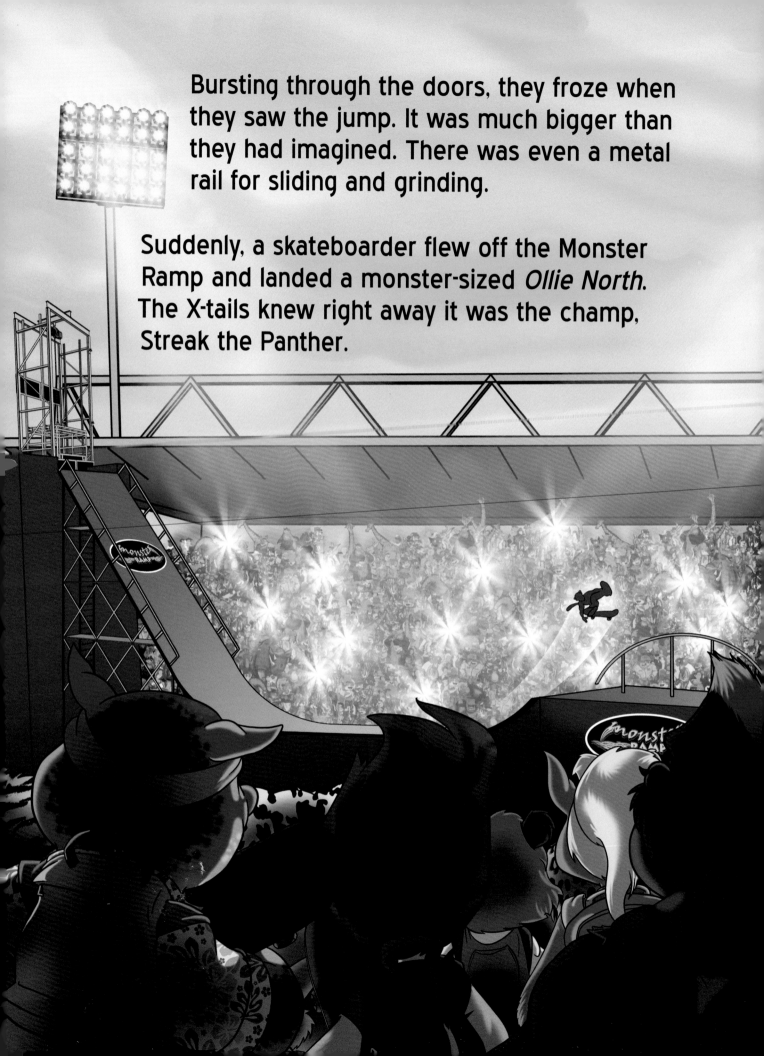

Bursting through the doors, they froze when they saw the jump. It was much bigger than they had imagined. There was even a metal rail for sliding and grinding.

Suddenly, a skateboarder flew off the Monster Ramp and landed a monster-sized *Ollie North*. The X-tails knew right away it was the champ, Streak the Panther.

Streak took off his helmet and flashed a smile and wink at the X-tails. Although he looked like an ordinary panther with glowing yellow eyes, Streak was anything but ordinary. He never wore a shirt, proudly showing off the lightning bolt of white fur on his chest.

"Wow, Streak is zoober-cool!" said Charm the Kangaroo. "We don't have any chance of winning. He's too good."

"It's not about winning," said Wisdom. "It's about doing our best and having fun."

They nodded in agreement as they hurried to join the contest. Because they were late, each X-tail only had one chance to make it to the final round.

The Monster Ramp towered high above them—so high, the X-tails took an elevator to get to the top. Up there, they did their safety check. Putting on their helmets, elbow pads and knee pads, they were now ready for the biggest jump ever!

Crash the Hippo looked far down below. His voice trembling, he squeaked,

"GaaaWHoooomPHaaaa, who's going first?"

Dazzle the Bear bravely stepped forward.
"GRRRRR!"
she growled. "This jump looks zoober-awesome!"
Stepping onto her skateboard, she dropped in and
zoomed away. Her cheeks flapped, her eyes watered,
and the wind whistled in her ears.

The X-tails watched in worry.
Dazzle was going fast—too fast!

And do you know what happened?

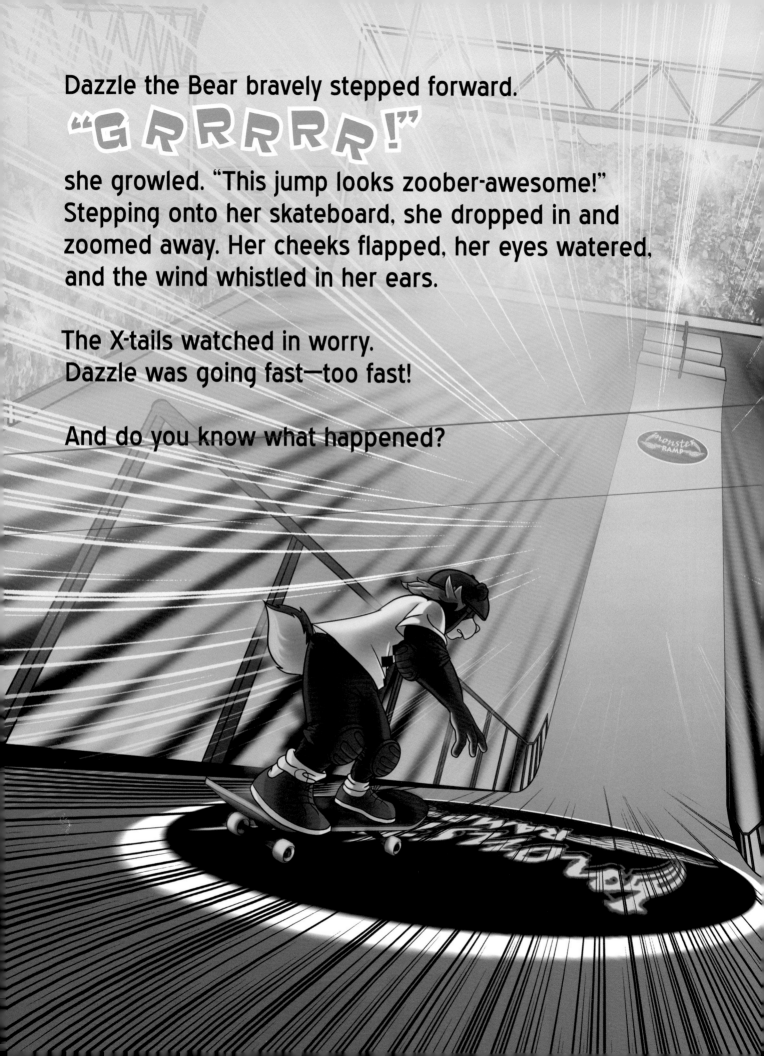

Dazzle lost control and accidentally did a *Double Front Flip.* She landed on her feet, but her skateboard was no where to be seen. Her cheeks turned red with embarrassment.

The crowd went bananas! Dazzle bowed and opened her mouth for her usual growl, but the only thing that came out was a big yawn. She slowly walked off the ramp.

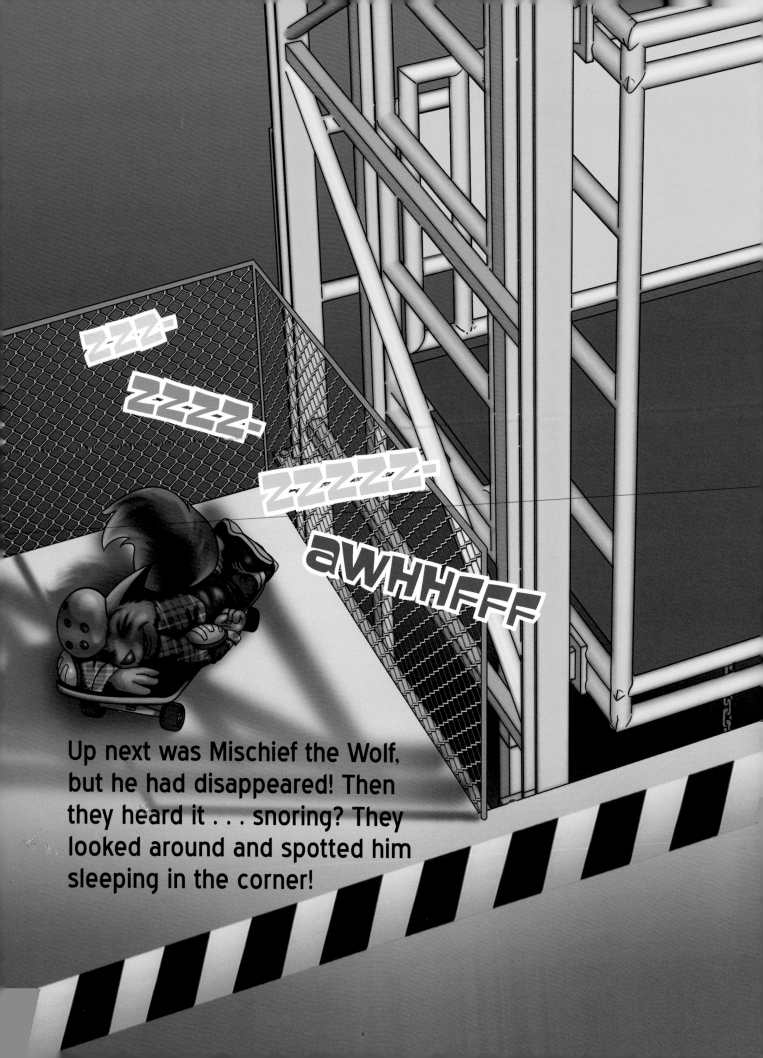

Up next was Mischief the Wolf, but he had disappeared! Then they heard it . . . snoring? They looked around and spotted him sleeping in the corner!

"Mischief, wake up!" yelled Flight the Gorilla.

Startled and confused, Mischief jumped onto his skateboard—and skated straight into the elevator! Before he realized his mistake, the door closed and down he went. Mischief had missed his turn.

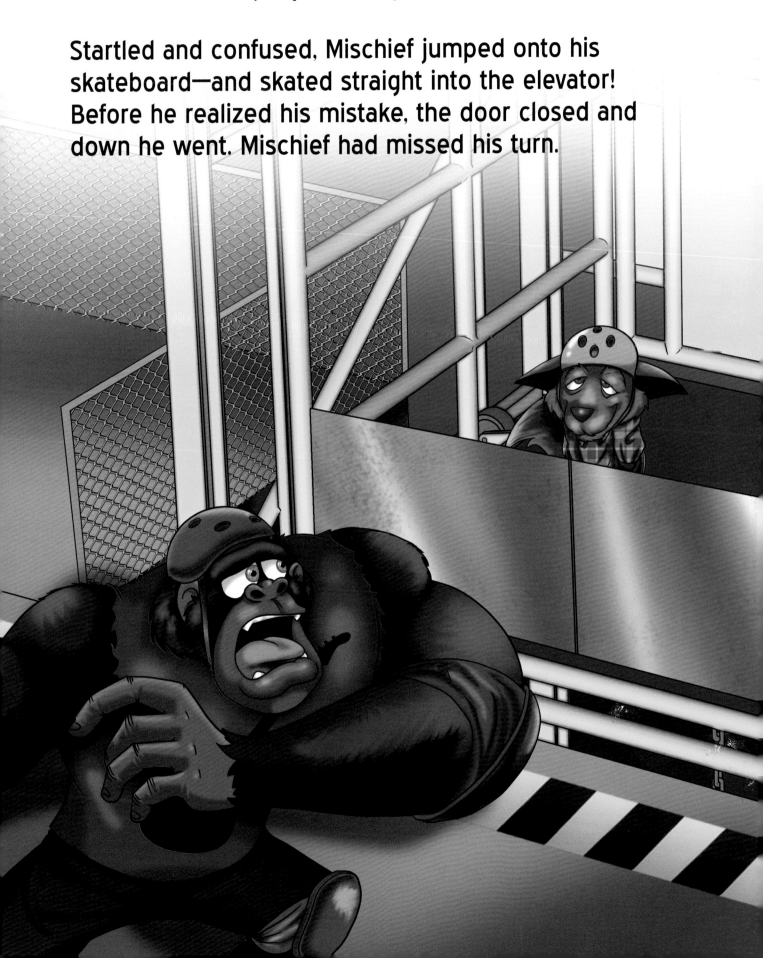

Things didn't get any better for the X-tails. Charm the Kangaroo, Flight the Gorilla, and Crash the Hippo all had zoober-spectacular wipe outs!

It was now Wisdom the Lion's turn.

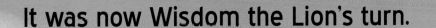

"ROOaaaRRRR!"

he thundered as he dropped in.

Like a rocket, he blasted into the air. His skateboard flipped under his feet and landed perfectly on top of the metal rail. He did a *Kickflip Boardslide*—the most difficult trick so far!

Wisdom had made it to the final round!

Rushing into the elevator, Wisdom joined the other three finalists at the top of the Monster Ramp.

A rastafarian rabbit and a purple-haired panda started the final round with zoober-amazing tricks:

SEVEN-TWENTY STALE FISH

and an

AIR WALK.

It was shaping up to be a classic showdown!

Next to go was Streak the Panther. With his famous
smile and wink to the crowd, he prepared to drop in,
but stopped and stepped off his skateboard. "Uh oh,"
he said, "my skateboard has a crack in it! If I go off
the jump, it will break and I could be hurt!"

Wisdom watched the clock. Streak was running
out of time! He was going to miss his turn!

Wisdom knew what he had to do. He ran
over to Streak and gave him his skateboard.

Streak couldn't believe his eyes. With one second left,
he smiled and dropped in. He crouched low and his fur
blew straight back. He launched off the Monster Ramp!

His skateboard slowly flipped in the air. He reached to grab his board, but missed! The crowd covered their eyes in fear. He tried again, and this time, he grabbed it! He held on tight and landed a *Heelflip Melon!*

The stadium erupted in cheers!

Then the crowd's attention turned to Wisdom, who stood alone without a skateboard. Seeing that her friend was in trouble, Charm the Kangaroo hopped into the elevator. The clock ticked down— thirty seconds . . . twenty seconds . . . ten seconds.

Suddenly, the elevator door opened and Charm threw her skateboard. In one swift motion, Wisdom caught it and jumped into the ramp.

The crowd gasped—he was going backwards!

And do you know what happened?

Wisdom used his zoober-cat balance and soared off the Monster Ramp. With brilliance and silky smooth style, he landed a *Switch Back Flip Indy!* The crowd went nuts and then became silent. Who had won?

The judges huddled together. Time
seemed to stop. After lots of whispering
back and forth, the judges made their decision.

Presented with a shiny gold medal,
Wisdom was the winner!

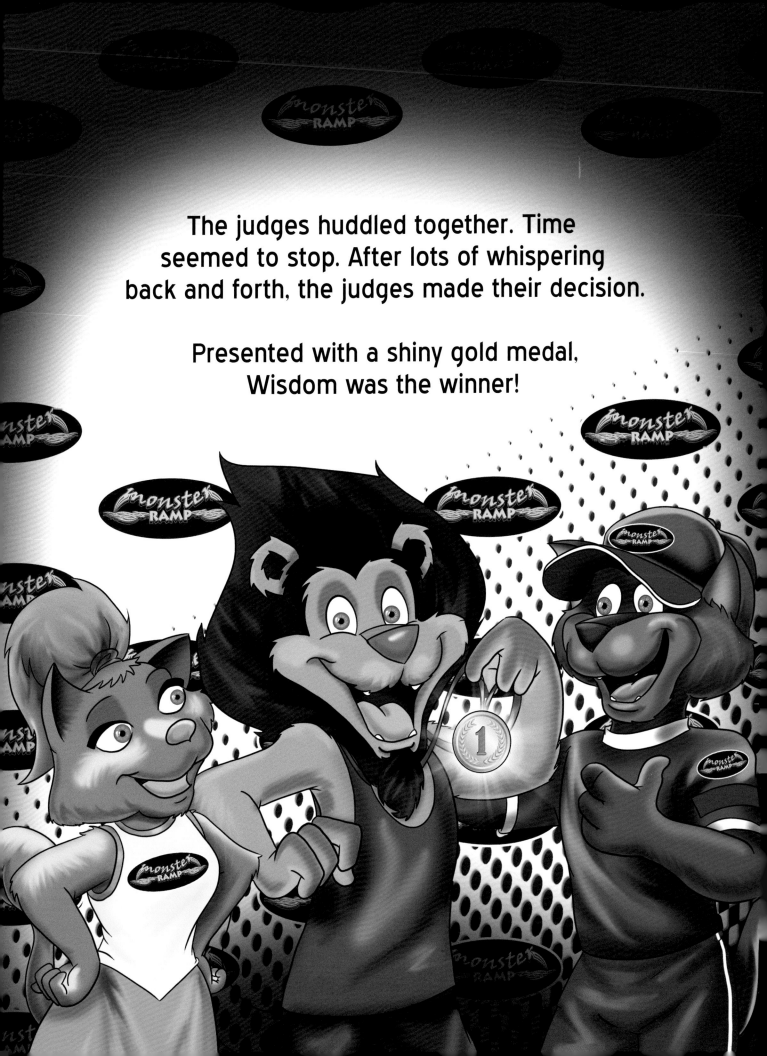

Streak was first to congratulate him. "Thank you so much for sharing your skateboard with me. You deserved to win. Your tricks were zoober-sweet!" Streak raised Wisdom's paw high into the air while the crowd cheered.

The rest of the X-tails joined the celebration, giving hugs and high-fives to all!

After the contest, they were driving home when Flight the Gorilla spoke up. "The only one to skateboard well today was Wisdom. What happened to the rest of us?"

The smart lion knew the answer, but stayed quiet.

"It was my fault," said Mischief. "My howling kept everyone awake. I've learned my lesson, and from now on, I'll control my excitement. Do you forgive me?"

"Of course!" answered the X-tails happily.

The X-van soon became silent. Most of the X-tails were falling asleep when Mischief rubbed his tummy. "Is anyone hungry? I can't wait to eat! I'm zoober-excited for some yummy food!"

"a-a-a-aaaaWHOOOOO!"

he howled.

The X-tails rolled their eyes and burst out laughing. Wisdom smiled fondly at his best friends.

# THE TRICK-TIONARY

## OLLIE NORTH

Almost every skateboard trick starts with an ollie. With the back foot, the skateboarder snaps the tail of the board hard on the ground and jumps at the same time. The result is an ollie when the skateboard pops into the air. After you learn this important trick, try to ollie and kick your front foot into the air like a kung-fu panda. You just did an Ollie North!

## BOARDSLIDE

Starting with an ollie, the skateboarder slides sideways along the center of the board on a slippery obstacle such as a rail. If you want to set the world record for longest boardslide, the secret is to rub wax on the rail—you'll slide forever!

# aiRWaLK

After launching into the air, the skateboarder grabs the nose of the skateboard and kicks out their legs in opposite directions. With this trick, you don't need to be an astronaut to walk on air!

# DOUBLE FRONT FLIP

A flip performed in a forward motion where the skateboarder rotates two times upside down. Even though Dazzle the Bear didn't land this trick in the Monster Ramp Contest, she never gave up. With lots of practice and the help of her gymnastics skills, she can now land it every time!

# HEELFLIP MELON

Starting with an ollie, the skateboarder kicks out the heel of their front foot toward the toe side edge of the skateboard. While the board flips underneath the skateboarder's feet, the front hand reaches behind and between the feet to grab the skateboard. After you land this trick, make sure to roll away with a big smile!

# KICKFLIP

Starting with an ollie, the skateboarder kicks out the toes of their front foot toward the heel side edge of the skateboard. The board will flip underneath the skateboarder's feet. Always remember to bend your knees when landing and to rooaaarrrr like Wisdom the Lion when you ride away like a champ!

# MANUAL

This trick may look simple, but don't be fooled! While rolling, the skateboarder lifts the front wheels into the air and doesn't let the tail touch the ground. The goal is to hold the front wheels in the air for as long as possible. After you learn this trick, ask Crash the Hippo how to do a One-footed Manual!

# POWERSLIDE

This trick is a fun way to slow down if you're going too fast. Using zoober-strength like Flight the Gorilla, the skateboarder turns the board sideways to slide all four wheels along the ground. Be careful—this trick is trickier than it looks!

## SEVEN-TWENTY STALEFISH

Starting with a monster-sized air, the skateboarder spins two full rotations. In the middle of the rotation, the back hand reaches behind and around the back leg to grab the skateboard. And don't worry if you're not a fan of stale fish—this trick isn't too smelly!

## SWITCH BACK FLIP INDY

A trick for experts only! Rolling backwards or switch, a flip is performed in a backward motion where the skateboarder rotates upside down. Once in the air, the back hand reaches in front and between the feet to grab the skateboard. So far, Wisdom is the only X-tail to land this trick!

# L.A. FIELDING

is an author of children's literature, and a member of the Canadian Authors Association. He dreamed up the X-tails for his two children, while telling stories on their long distance trips to the mountains each winter weekend. It is his family's cozy log home in Prince George, British Columbia, and their Fielding Shred Shack at a local ski resort, where he draws his inspiration.

Growing up skateboarding, biking, and snowboarding, L.A. Fielding now shares the fun of those sports with his family. When not writing or telling stories, he focuses his thoughts on forestry as a Registered Professional Forester. *The X-tails Skateboard at Monster Ramp* is his second book in the X-tails series.

Other books in the series include:

- *The X-tails Ski at Spider Ridge*
- *The X-tails BMX at Thunder Track*
- *The X-tails Heli-Ski at Blue Paw Mountain*
- *The X-tails Surf at Shark Bay*
- *The X-tails Mountain Bike at Rattlesnake Mountain*
- *The X-tails Snowboard at Shred Park*

CHECK OUT  aT WWW.THEXTAILS.COM